PASSIN' GAS IN CLASS

PASSIN' GAS IN CLASS

Corrin Haskell

Illustrations by Marlon Sagana Ingram

ABOOKS

Alive Book Publishing

Additional copies may be ordered from the publisher for educational, business,
promotional or premium use. For information, contact ALIVE Book Publishing at:
alivebookpublishing.com, or call (925) 837-7303.

Book Design by Alex Johnson

ISBN 13
978-1-63132-148-1 Harcover
978-1-63132-147-4 Paperback

Library of Congress Control Number: 2021916779
Library of Congress Cataloging-in-Publication Data is available upon request.

First Edition

Published in the United States of America by ALIVE Book Publishing and
ALIVE Publishing Group, imprints of Advanced Publishing LLC
3200 A Danville Blvd., Suite 204, Alamo, California 94507
alivebookpublishing.com

Printed in the United States of America
10 9 8 7 6 5 4 3 2 1

This Book is dedicated to the students
of Brookfield Elementary
and the whole Brookfield Village Community.

This story is based on actual conversations my students and I
have had over the past 25 years of my teaching 5th grade.
For some reason, the first classroom fart was a major event
in the class each year. Students reacted in different ways
over those 25 years, and this book is about the many lively
conversations we had in the classroom.
Enjoy!

It was the first day of 5th grade and little Ricky was nervous.
As he sat in class and listened to the teacher
introduce herself and explain the rules of the class,
Ricky felt his stomach bubble.
This often happened when he got nervous. He gets gas.

Oh-NO! Suddenly he felt it. A fart. It was inching ever closer to releasing itself, which would create a loud noise, followed by the horrible smell that would leave the class in total chaos. Ricky would be the laughing stock of the class. He knew if he farted in class (on the first day), he would be labeled "Gas God," "Icky Ricky," or "Fart-A-Saurus" for the rest of the year. He thought deeply about his next move.

He thought back to a "fart speech" his favorite teacher, Mr. Brooks, had given last year. It outlined "proper classroom farting etiquette" to avoid chaos and embarrassment...

Option 1: The "Lean and Squeeze." Everyone who has ever farted in a classroom knows that when the fart is released against those hard plastic chairs, a very explosive "BOOM" sound occurs. So one must lean to the side and slowly release the fart as gently as possible. Then, quickly go back to a normal seating position so nobody notices and to trap the smell under your body. This works well, unless you have stinky gas...which leads to option 2.

Option 2: The "Fart Walk." In this case, you simply ask to be excused to go to the bathroom or office, then go for a walk down the hall, or outside, depending on how your school is designed. Be sure to walk far away from the classroom before releasing, then let it out and "fan it off" as you walk back, because we all know those super stinky ones can travel and follow you back to class.

Option 3: "Cause a Distraction." This is a classic method. Once you feel the release about to happen, simply create some type of distraction. Ideas include: faking a sneeze or cough, dropping a book or something, or simply asking "What IS that?"
in a loud voice, balling up some paper in an obnoxiously loud way, etc. You get the point.
Once the class is preoccupied by the distraction...
Let 'er rip!

Option 4: The "Blame Game." When you have no other option, simply deny and shift the blame to someone else. We have all been guilty of this at some point. To use this method you have to be the first one to notice, or at least mention, the fart. Don't worry, the ole' "whoever smelt it, dealt it" argument is old and out-dated. Once you are sure that several of your fellow students are aware of the fart (by recognizing facial expressions, nose holds, mouth covering, or faces of disgust and bewilderment), then simply choose a poor soul and then yell out, "EWW Jason (choose a name)! That STINKS! GROSS!! UGGGGH." This will place all the focus on the accused and you will be free from blame. If they try to turn it around and blame you, then simply say, "Wasn't me," and flat out deny it.

Suddenly, while Ricky was deep in thought, it happened. "NO!" The fart released itself, but luckily, no one noticed... yet. As the culprit, you are always the first one to smell it. Dang! It was bad. He started to notice the other kids having fits about the smell. Eventually one of them exclaimed, "UMMMM, who farted? CUZ IT STIIIINNNKKKKS!" and dramatically fell out of the chair. Utter chaos followed with students gagging, coughing, flailing about in all kinds of ways. However, fortunately nobody blamed Ricky. "Whew, I'm safe," he thought.

So the teacher had no choice but to jump in and and calm the class down. "Settle down class. Calm down," said Ms. Chelsea. "Now I realize a classroom fart can be a very exciting event for 5th graders, but I am not sure why." She then passed out a piece of paper to everyone and had them write down why a classroom fart got them so excited?

The girls in the class were not amused. "This is gross," said Jasmine. "It doesn't get me excited... it gets me nauseous." Many girls in the class agreed and simply wrote, "there is nothing exciting about farts," in a variety of ways.

The boys, however, had lots to say. Some of their responses included: "Fart smells can distract me from my work. How can we concentrate?" "The loud noise can be startling." "Farters have power!" "Mr. Brooks told us proper classroom farting etiquette last year—WHAT HAPPENED?" "Big fart = healthy heart,"and on and on.

The teacher quietly read each response before passing the papers back to students.
"Ok class," she said, "I think we need to have a talk."
Eye-roll.

"Everybody farts," Ms. Chelsea started out, "in many different ways. No one can control when or where they fart. It is natural and part of daily life. However, just like there are different kinds of everything in this world, there are different kind of farts." "Let's Discuss," said Jimmy. "Okay," said Ms. Chelsea, "anyone have any suggestions?" "Uh, what exactly are we talking about Ms. Chelsea?" questioned Jasmine. "FARTS," yelled Michael. "I know one kind. Silent but Violent! (the obvious one)." "Yes, correct," said Ms. Chelsea, "that is probably the most commonly known–a classic. The no-noise, big- stink type. Anyone else?"

The girls all looked at each other with astonished faces. "I can't believe this," Jasmine said. The boys, however, got all excited. "Girls don't fart anyways," said Michael, "they just fluff." "Loud and Proud. Like when you just don't care and fire away," yelled Maurice. "Repeat, rapid fire," said Phil, "like when you are running and fart with each step. That can be fun!"

The boys went on and on. Ms. Chelsea sensed the girls discomfort and brought the discussion to a close. "I want everyone to write down WHY you think we have different farts and if you'd like, which one is your favorite and why?" The kids all wrote down their responses and turned them in before lining up for lunch.

Ricky was one of the last ones to turn his in. He sat there taking his time and had almost forgotten that it was his fart that set off this whole conversation. Ricky smiled and thought, "I don't think the students will ever forget the 'lesson of the day,' or Ms. Chelsea's use of a teachable moment."

PASSIN' GAS IN CLASS

CORRIN HASKELL

Born and raised in Seattle, Washington, Corrin Haskell moved to Oakland, California in the mid-nineties to pursue a teaching career after graduating from University of Washington. He has been teaching 5th grade at Brookfield Elementary in Oakland, California for the past 25 years. He also coaches a variety of sports teams and is involved with many community programs near the school. Corrin was recently recognized as an "All-Star Educator" by the NBA Cares program and has worked with the Learn Fresh non-profit education company. Aside from his work in education, for two decades, Corrin founded and ran the reggae/dancehall record label, Lustre Kings Productions, before moving into the world of children's literature. Passin' Gas in Class is his second children's book. Corrin's debut book, The Water Hole, was published in 2020 (also by ALIVE Book Publishing). Corrin has written, and plans to release, many more children's books in the coming years.

MARLON INGRAM

Located in the San Francisco Bay Area, Marlon has designed and produced client projects within the art, design, and education industries for over 20 years. He is a multidisciplinary thinker who focuses on art, design, and informative exhibitions. Marlon's production style is based upon processes found in apparel design, typography, and video production. His work was recognized in SF Weekly's "Top 5th Element Teachers" in 2008, and in the Yerba Buena Center of the Arts for the "YBCA's 100 Top Culture Makers" award, in 2015. Aside from his design work, Marlon was the stunt skater-actor for the lead role in the movie, "The Last Blackman in San Francisco," which won SF Film Festival and Cannes awards. He also created motion graphics for, "When We Gather," a film that celebrates the historic achievements of women whose efforts led to the election of the first female Vice President of the United States.

A BOOKS

ALIVE Book Publishing and ALIVE Publishing Group
are imprints of Advanced Publishing LLC,
3200 A Danville Blvd., Suite 204, Alamo, California 94507

Telephone: 925.837.7303
alivebookpublishing.com

CPSIA information can be obtained
at www.ICGtesting.com
Printed in the USA
BVHW022353191021
619340BV00001B/1